Castes in India

Bhimrao Ramji Ambedkar

DIAMOND BOOKS

Publisher : **Diamond Pocket Books (P) Ltd.**
X-30, Okhla Industrial Area, Phase-II
New Delhi-110020
Phone : 011- 40712200
E-mail : sales@dpb.in
Website : www.diamondbook.in

Castes in India

By - *Bhimrao Ramji Ambedkar*

About the Author

Bhimrao Ramji Ambedkar (1891-1956) was India's most popular leader of the Dalits. He was also the Union Law Minister of the Government of India during 1947–51. Although born in a Dalit Mahar family, he was awarded a scholarship by the Gaekwar (ruler) of Baroda and he studied at universities in the US, the UK, and Germany. Deeply pained at ill-treatment of Dalits, Ambedkar turned to legal practice and to teaching. n his early career, he was an economist, professor, and lawyer. His later life was marked by his political activities; he became involved in campaigning and negotiations for India's independence, publishing journals, advocating political rights and social freedom for Dalits, and contributing significantly to the establishment of the state of India.

Ambedkar soon established his leadership among Dalits, founded several journals on their behalf, and succeeded in obtaining special representation for them in the legislative councils of the government. He took a leading part in the framing of the Indian Constitution, outlawing discrimination against untouchables, and skillfully helped to steer it through the assembly. In October 1956, he renounced

Hinduism and became a Buddhist, together with about 200,000 fellow Dalits, at a ceremony in Nagpur.

Castes in India

Their mechanism, genesis and development.[1]

BY BHIMRAO R. AMBEDKAR, M. A.

Many of us, I dare say, have witnessed local, national, or international expositions of material objects that make up the sum total of human civilization. But few can entertain the idea of there being such a thing as an exposition of human institutions. Exhibition of human institutions is a strange idea; some might call it the wildest of ideas. But as students of Ethnology I hope you will not be hard on this innovation, for it is not so, and to you at least it should not be strange.

You all have visited, I believe, some historic place like the ruins of Pompeii, and listened with curiosity to the history of the remains as it flowed from the glib tongue of the guide. In my opinion a student of Ethnology, in one sense at least, is much like the guide. Like his prototype, he holds up (perhaps with more seriousness and desire of self instruction) the social institutions to view, with all the objectiveness humanly possible, and inquires into their origin and function.

---

[1] A paper read before the Anthropology Seminar (9th May 1916) of Dr. A. A. Goldenweiser, Columbia University, New York.

Most of our fellow students in this Seminar, which concerns itself with Primitive *versus* Modern Society, have ably acquitted themselves along these lines by giving lucid expositions of the various institutions, modern or primitive, in which they are interested. It is my turn now, this evening, to entertain you, as best I can, with a paper on "Castes in India: their mechanism, genesis and development."

I need hardly remind you of the complexity of the subject I intend to handle. Subtler minds and abler pens than mine have been brought to the task of unravelling the mysteries of Caste; but unfortunately it still remains in the domain of the "unexplained," not to say of the "un-understood." I am quite alive to the complex intricacies of a hoary institution like Caste, but I am not so pessimistic as to relegate it to the region of the unknowable, for I believe it can be known. The caste problem is a vast one, both theoretically and practically. Practically, it is an institution that portends tremendous consequences. It is a local problem, but one capable of much wider mischief, for "as long as caste in India does exist, Hindus will hardly intermarry or have any social intercourse with outsiders; and if Hindus migrate to other regions on earth, Indian caste would become a world problem."[2] Theoretically, it has defied a great many scholars who have taken upon themselves, as a labour of love, to dig into its origin. Such being the case, I cannot treat the problem in its entirety. Time,

---

2 Ketkar, Caste, p. 4.

space and acumen, I am afraid, would all fail me, if I attempted to do otherwise than limit myself to a phase of it, namely, the genesis, mechanism and spread of the caste system. I will strictly observe this rule, and will dwell on extraneous matters only when it is necessary to clarify or support a point in my thesis.

To proceed with the subject. According to well-known ethnologists, the population of India is a mixture of Aryans, Dravidians, Mongolians and Scythians. All these stocks of people came into India from various directions and with various cultures, centuries ago, when they were in a tribal state. They all in turn elbowed their entry into the country by fighting with their predecessors, and after a stomachful of it settled down as peaceful neighbours. Through constant contact and mutual intercourse they evolved a common [pg 82] culture that superseded their distinctive cultures. It may be granted that there has not been a thorough amalgamation of the various stocks that make up the peoples of India, and to a traveller from within the boundaries of India the East presents a marked contrast in physique and even in colour to the West, as does the South to the North. But amalgamation can never be the sole criterion of homogeneity as predicated of any people. Ethnically all peoples are heterogeneous. It is the unity of culture that is the basis of homogeneity. Taking this for granted, I venture to say that there is no country that can rival the Indian Peninsula with respect to the unity of its culture. It has not only a geographic unity, but it has over and above all a deeper and a much more fundamental unity—the indubitable cultural unity that covers the land from end to end. But it is because of this homogeneity that Caste becomes a problem so difficult to be explained. If the Hindu Society were a mere federation of mutually exclusive units, the matter would be simple enough. But Caste is a parcelling of an already homogeneous unit, and the explanation of the genesis of Caste is the explanation of this process of parcelling.

Before launching into our field of enquiry, it is better to advise ourselves regarding the nature of a caste. I will therefore draw upon a few of the best students of caste for their definitions of it.

(1) M. Senart, a French authority, defines a caste as "a close corporation, in theory at any rate rigorously hereditary: equipped with a certain traditional and independent organisation, including a chief and a council, meeting on occasion in assemblies of more or less plenary authority and joining together at certain festivals: bound together by common occupations, which relate more particularly to marriage and to food and to questions of ceremonial pollution, and ruling its members by the exercise of jurisdiction, the extent of which varies, but which succeeds in making the authority of the community more felt by the sanction of certain penalties and, above all, by final irrevocable exclusion from the group."

(2) Mr. Nesfield defines a caste as "a class of the community which disowns any connection with any other class and can neither intermarry nor eat nor drink with any but persons of their own community."

(3) According to Sir H. Risley, "a caste may be defined as a collection of families or groups of families bearing a common name which usually denotes or is associated, with specific occupation, claiming common descent from a mythical ancestor, human or divine, professing to follow the same professional callings and are regarded by those who are competent to give an opinion as forming a single homogeneous community."

(4) Dr. Ketkar defines caste as "a social group having two characteristics: (1) membership is confined to those who are born of members and includes all persons so born; (2) the members are forbidden by an inexorable social law to marry outside the group."

To review these definitions is of great importance for our purpose. It will be noticed that taken individually the definitions of three of the writers include too much or too little: none is complete or correct by itself and all have missed the central point in the mechanism of the Caste system. Their mistake lies in trying to define caste as an isolated unit by itself, and not as a group within, and with definite relations to, the system of caste as a whole. Yet collectively all of them are complementary to one another, each one emphasising what has been obscured in the other. By way of criticism, therefore, I will take only those points common to all Castes in each of the above definitions which are regarded as peculiarities of Caste and evaluate them as such.

[pg 83] To start with M. Senart, He draws attention to the "idea of pollution" as a characteristic of Caste. With regard to this point it may be safely said that it is by no means a peculiarity of Caste as such. It usually originates in priestly ceremonialism and is a particular case of the general belief in purity. Consequently its necessary connection with Caste may be completely denied without damaging the working of Caste. The "idea of pollution" has been attached to the institution of Caste, only because the Caste that enjoys the highest rank is the priestly Caste: while we know that priest and purity are old associates. We may therefore conclude that the "idea of pollution" is a characteristic of Caste only in so far as Caste has a religious flavour. Mr. Nesfield in his way dwells on the absence of messing with those outside the Caste as one of its characteristics. In spite of the newness of the point we must say that Mr. Nesfield has mistaken the effect for the cause. Caste, being a self-enclosed unit, naturally limits social intercourse, including messing etc., to members within it. Consequently this absence of messing with outsiders is not due to positive prohibition, but is a natural result of Caste, *i.e.*, exclusiveness. No doubt this absence of messing, originally due to exclusiveness, acquired the prohibitory character of a religious injunction, but it may be regarded as a later growth. Sir H. Risley, makes no new point deserving of special attention.

We now pass on to the definition of Dr. Ketkar, who has done much for the elucidation of the subject. Not only is he a native, but he has also brought a critical acumen and an open mind to bear on his study of Caste. His definition merits consideration, for he has defined Caste in its relation to a system of Castes, and has concentrated his attention only on those characteristics which are absolutely necessary for the existence of a Caste within a system, rightly excluding all others as being secondary or derivative in character. With respect to his definition it must, however, be said that in it there is a slight confusion of thought, lucid and clear as otherwise it is. He speaks of **Prohibition of Intermarriage** and **Membership by Autogeny** as the two characteristics of Caste. I submit that these are but two aspects of one and the same thing, and not two different things as Dr. Ketkar supposes them to be. If you prohibit inter-marriage the result is that you limit, membership to those born within the group. Thus the two are the obverse and the reverse sides of the same medal.

This critical evaluation of the various characteristics of Caste leaves no doubt that prohibition, or rather the absence of intermarriage—endogamy, to be concise—is the only one that can be called the essence of Caste when rightly understood. But some may deny this on abstract anthropological grounds, for there exist endogamous groups without giving rise to the problem of Caste. In a general way this may be true, as endogamous societies, culturally different, making their abode in localities more or less removed, and having little to do with each other, are a physical reality. The negroes and the whites and the various tribal groups that go by the name of American Indians in the United States may be cited as more or less appropriate illustrations in support of this view. But we must not confuse matters, for in India the situation is different. As pointed out before, the peoples of India form a homogeneous whole. The various races of India occupying definite territories have more or less fused into one another and do possess a cultural unity, which is the only criterion of a homogeneous population. Given this homogeneity as a basis, Caste becomes a problem altogether new in character and wholly absent in the situation constituted by the mere propinquity of endogamous social or tribal [pg 84] groups. Caste in India means an artificial chopping off of the population into fixed and definite units, each one prevented from fusing into another through the custom of endogamy. Thus the conclusion is inevitable that **endogamy is the only characteristic that is peculiar to Caste**, and if we succeed in showing how endogamy is maintained, we shall practically have proved the genesis and also the mechanism of Caste.

It may not be quite easy for you to anticipate why I regard endogamy as a key to the mystery of the Caste system. Not to strain your imagination too much, I will proceed to give you my reasons for it.

It may not also be out of place to emphasize at this moment that no civilized society of to-day presents more survivals of primitive times than does the Indian society. Its religion is essentially primitive and its tribal code, in spite of the advance of time and civilization, operates in all its pristine vigour even to-day. One of these primitive survivals, to which I wish particularly to draw your attention, is the **custom of exogamy**. The prevalence of exogamy in the primitive world is a fact too well known to need any explanation. With the growth of history, however, exogamy has lost its efficacy and, excepting the nearest blood-kins, there is usually no social bar restricting the field of marriage. But regarding the peoples of India the law of exogamy is a positive injunction even to-day. Indian society still savours of the clan system, even though there are no clans: and this can be easily seen from the law of matrimony which centres round the principle of exogamy, for it is not that *sapindas* (blood-kins) cannot marry, but a marriage even between *sagotras* (of the same class) is regarded as a sacrilege.

Nothing is therefore more important for you to remember than the fact that endogamy is foreign to the people of India. The various *gotras* of India are and have been exogamous: so are the other groups with totemic organization. It is no exaggeration to say that with the people of India exogamy is a creed and none dare infringe it, so much so that, in spite of the endogamy of the Castes within them, exogamy is strictly observed and that there are more rigorous penalties for violating exogamy than there are for violating endogamy. You will, therefore, readily see that with exogamy as the rule there could be no Castes, for exogamy means fusion. But we *have* Castes; consequently in the final analysis creation of Castes, so far as India is concerned, means the superposition of endogamy on exogamy. However, in an originally exogamous population an easy working out of endogamy (which is equivalent to the creation of Caste) is a grave problem, and it is in the consideration of the means utilized for the preservation of endogamy against exogamy that we may hope to find the solution of our problem.

Thus the **superposition of endogamy on exogamy means the creation of Caste**. But this is not an easy affair. Let us take an imaginary group that desires to make itself into a Caste and analyse what means it will have to adopt to make itself endogamous. If a group desires to make itself endogamous a formal injunction against intermarriage with outside groups will be of no avail, especially if prior to the introduction of endogamy, exogamy had been the rule in all matrimonial relations. Again, there is a tendency in all groups lying in close contact with one another to assimilate and amalgamate, and thus consolidate into a homogenous society. If this tendency is to be strongly counteracted in the interest of Caste formation, it is absolutely necessary to circumscribe a circle outside which people should not contract marriages.

Nevertheless, this encircling to prevent marriages from without creates problems from within which are not very easy of solution. Roughly speaking, in a normal group the [pg 85] two sexes are more or less evenly distributed, and generally speaking there is an equality between those of the same age. The equality is, however, never quite realized in actual societies. At the same time to the group that is desirous of making itself into a caste the maintenance of equality between the sexes becomes the ultimate goal, for without it endogamy can no longer subsist. In other words, if endogamy is to be preserved conjugal rights from within have to be provided for, otherwise members of the group will be driven out of the circle to take care of themselves in any way they can. But in order that the conjugal rights be provided for from within, it is absolutely necessary to maintain a numerical equality between the marriageable units of the two sexes within the group desirous of making itself into a Caste. It is only through the maintenance of such an equality that the necessary endogamy of the group can be kept intact, and a very large disparity is sure to break it.

The problem of Caste, then, ultimately resolves itself into one of repairing the disparity between the marriageable units of the two sexes within it. Left to nature, the much needed parity between the units can be realized only when a couple dies simultaneously. But this is a rare contingency. The husband may die before the wife and create a *surplus woman*, who must be disposed of, else through intermarriage she will violate the endogamy of the group. In like manner the husband may survive his wife and be a *surplus man*, whom the group, while it may sympathise with him for the sad bereavement, has to dispose of, else he will marry outside the Caste and will break the endogamy. Thus both the *surplus man* and the *surplus woman* constitute a menace to the Caste if not taken care of, for not finding suitable partners inside their prescribed circle (and left to themselves they cannot find any, for if the matter be not regulated there can only be just enough pairs to go round) very likely they will transgress the boundary, marry outside and import offspring that is foreign to the Caste.

Let us see what our imaginary group is likely to do with this *surplus man* and *surplus woman*. We will first take up the case of the *surplus woman*. She can be disposed of in two different ways so as to preserve the endogamy of the Caste.

First: burn her on the funeral pyre of her deceased husband and get rid of her. This, however, is rather an impracticable way of solving the problem of sex disparity. In some cases it may work, in others it may not. Consequently every *surplus woman* cannot thus be disposed of, because it is an easy solution but a hard realization. And so the *surplus woman* (= widow), if not disposed of, remains in the group: but in her very existence lies a double danger. She may marry outside the Caste and violate endogamy, or she may marry within the Caste and through competition encroach upon the chances of marriage that must be reserved for the potential brides in the Caste. She is therefore a menace in any case, and something must be done to her if she cannot be burned along with her deceased husband.

The second remedy is to enforce widowhood on her for the rest of her life. So far as the objective results are concerned, burning is a better solution than enforcing widowhood. Burning the widow eliminates all the three evils that a *surplus woman* is fraught with. Being dead and gone she creates no problem of remarriage either inside or outside the Caste. But compulsory widowhood is superior to burning because it is more practicable. Besides being comparatively humane it also guards against the evils of remarriage as does burning: but it fails to guard the morals of the group. No doubt under compulsory widowhood the woman remains, and just because she is deprived of her natural right of being a legitimate wife in future, the incentive to immoral conduct is increased. But [pg 86] this is by no means an insuperable difficulty. She can be degraded to a condition in which she is no longer a source of allurement.

The problem of *surplus man* (= widower) is much more important and much more difficult than that of the *surplus woman* in a group that desires to make itself into a Caste. From time immemorial man as compared with woman has had the upper hand. He is a dominant figure in every group and of the two sexes has greater prestige. With this traditional superiority of man over woman his wishes have always been consulted. Woman, on the other hand, has been an easy prey to all kinds of iniquitous injunctions, religious, social or economic. But man as a maker of injunctions is most often above them all. Such being the case, you cannot accord the same kind of treatment to a *surplus man* as you can to a *surplus woman* in a Caste.

The project of burning him with his deceased wife is hazardous in two ways: first of all it cannot be done, simply because he is a man. Secondly, if done, a sturdy soul is lost to the Caste. There remain then only two solutions which can conveniently dispose of him. I say conveniently, because he is an asset to the group.

Important as he is to the group, endogamy is still more important, and the solution must assure both these ends. Under these circumstances he may be forced, or I should say induced, after the manner of the widow, to remain a widower for the rest of his life. This solution is not altogether difficult, for without any compulsion some are so disposed as to enjoy self-imposed celibacy, or even to take a further step of their own accord and renounce the world and its joys. But, given human nature as it is, this solution can hardly be expected to be realized. On the other hand, as is very likely to be the case, if the *surplus man* remains in the group as an active participator in group activities, he is a danger to the morals of the group. Looked at from a different point of view celibacy, though easy in cases where it succeeds, is not so advantageous even then to the material prospects of the Caste. If he observes genuine celibacy and renounces the world, he would not be a menace to the preservation of Caste endogamy or Caste morals as he undoubtedly would be if he remained a secular person. But as an ascetic celibate he is as good as burned, so far as the material well-being of his Caste is concerned. A Caste, in order that it may be large enough to afford a vigorous communal life, must be maintained at a certain numerical strength. But to hope for this and to proclaim celibacy is the same as trying to cure atrophy by bleeding.

Imposing celibacy on the *surplus man* in the group, therefore, fails both theoretically and practically. It is in the interest of the Caste to keep him as a *grahastha* (one who raises a family), to use a Sanskrit technical term. But the problem is to provide him with a wife from within the Caste. At the outset this is not possible, for the ruling ratio in a caste has to be one man to one woman and none can have two chances of marriage, for in a Caste thoroughly self-enclosed there are always just enough marriageable women to go round for the marriageable men. Under these circumstances the *surplus man* can be provided with a wife only by recruiting a bride from the ranks of those not yet marriageable in order to tie him down to the group. This is certainly the best of the possible solutions in the case of the *surplus man*. By this, he is kept within the Caste. By this means numerical depletion through constant outflow is guarded against, and by this endogamy and morals are preserved.

It will now be seen that the four means by which numerical disparity between the two sexes is conveniently maintained are: (1) Burning the widow with her deceased [pg 87] husband; (2) Compulsory widowhood—a milder form of burning; (3) Imposing celibacy on the widower; (4) Wedding him to a girl not yet marriageable. Though, as I said above, burning the widow and imposing celibacy on the widower are of doubtful service to the group in its endeavour to preserve its endogamy, all of them operate as *means*. But means, as forces, when liberated or set in motion create an end. What then is the end that these means create? They create and perpetuate endogamy, while caste and endogamy, according to our analysis of the various definitions of caste, are one and the same thing. Thus the existence of these means is identical with caste and caste involves those means.

This, in my opinion, is the general mechanism of a caste in a system of castes. Let us now turn from these high generalities to the castes in Hindu society and inquire into their mechanism. I need hardly promise that there are a great many pitfalls in the path of those who try to unfold the past, and caste in India to be sure is a very ancient institution. This is especially true where there exist no authentic or written records, or where the people, like the Hindus, are so constituted that to them writing history is a folly, for the world is an illusion. But institutions do live, though for a long time they may remain unrecorded and as often as not customs and morals are like fossils that tell their own history. If this is true, our task will be amply rewarded if we scrutinize the solution the Hindus arrived at to meet the problems of the *surplus man* and *surplus woman*.

Complex though it be in its general working the Hindu Society, even to a superficial observer, presents three singular uxorial customs, namely:—

1. *Sati* or the burning of the widow on the funeral pyre of her deceased husband.
2. Enforced widowhood by which a widow is not allowed to remarry.
3. Girl marriage.

In addition, one also notes a great hankering after *sannyasa* (renunciation) on the part of the widower, but this may in some cases be due purely to psychic disposition.

So far as I know, no scientific explanation of the origin of these customs is forthcoming even to-day. We have plenty of philosophy to tell us why these customs were honoured, but nothing to tell us the causes of their origin and existence. *Sati* has been honoured (*Cf.* A. K. Coomaraswamy, *Sati: a Defence of the Eastern Woman* in the *British Sociological Review*, Vol. VI. 1913) because it is a "proof of the perfect unity of body and soul" between husband and wife and of "devotion beyond the grave;" because it embodied the ideal of wifehood, which is well expressed by Umâ when she said "Devotion to her Lord is woman's honour, it is her eternal heaven: and O Maheshvara," she adds with a most touching human cry, "I desire not paradise itself if thou art not satisfied with me!" Why compulsory widowhood is honoured I know not, nor have I yet met with any one who sang in praise of it, though there are a great many who adhere to it. The eulogy in honour of girl marriage is reported by Dr. Ketkar to be as follows: "A really faithful man or woman ought not to feel affection for a woman or a man other than the one with whom he or she is united. Such purity is compulsory not only after marriage, but even before marriage, for that is the only correct ideal of chastity. No maiden could be considered pure if she feels love for a man other than the one to whom she might be married. As she does not know to whom she is going to be married, she must not feel affection for any man at all before marriage. If she does so, it is a sin. So it is better for a girl to know whom she has to love, before any sexual consciousness has been awakened in her."[3] Hence girl marriage.

---

[3] History of Caste in India, 1909, pp. 32–33.

This high-flown and ingenious sophistry indicates why these institutions were honoured, but does not tell us why they were practised. My own interpretation is that they were honoured because they were practised. Any one slightly acquainted with rise of individualism in the 18th century will appreciate my remark. At all times, it is the movement that is most important; and the philosophies grow around it long afterwards to justify it and give it a moral support. In like manner I urge that the very fact that these customs were so highly eulogized proves that they needed eulogy for their prevalence. Regarding the question as to why they arose, I submit that they were needed to create the structure of caste and the philosophies in honour of them were intended to popularize them, or to gild the pill, as we might say, for they must have been so abominable and shocking to the moral sense of the unsophisticated that they needed a great deal of sweetening. These customs are essentially of the nature of *means*, though they are represented as ideals. But this should not blind us from understanding the *results* that flow from them. One might safely say that idealization of means is necessary and in this particular case was perhaps motivated to endow them with greater efficacy. Calling a means an end does no harm, except that it disguises its real character; but it does not deprive it of its real nature, that of a means. You may pass a law that all cats are dogs, just as you can call a means an end. But you can no more change the nature of means thereby than you can turn cats into dogs; consequently I am justified in holding that, whether regarded as ends or as means, *Sati*, *enforced widowhood* and *girl marriage* are customs that were primarily intended to solve the problem of the *surplus man* and *surplus woman* in a caste and to maintain its endogamy. Strict endogamy could not be preserved without these customs, while caste without endogamy is a fake.

Having explained the mechanism of the creation and preservation of Caste in India, the further question as to its genesis naturally arises. The question of origin is always an annoying question and in the study of Caste it is sadly neglected: some have connived at it, while others have dodged it. Some are puzzled as to whether there could be such a thing as the origin of caste and suggest that "if we cannot control our fondness for the word 'origin', we should better use the plural form, *viz.*, 'origins of caste'." As for myself I do not feel puzzled by the Origin of Caste in India, for, as I have established before, endogamy is the only characteristic of Caste and when I say **origin of caste** I mean **the origin of the mechanism for endogamy**.

The atomistic conception of individuals in a Society so greatly popularised—I was about to say vulgarized—in political orations is the greatest humbug. To say that individuals make up society is trivial; society is always composed of classes. It may be an exaggeration to assert the theory of class-conflict, but the existence of definite classes in a society is a fact. Their basis may differ. They may be economic or intellectual or social, but an individual in a society is always a member of a class. This is a universal fact and early Hindu society could not have been an exception to this rule, and, as a matter of fact, we know it was not. If we bear this generalization in mind, our study of the genesis of caste would be very much facilitated, for we have only to determine what was the class that first made itself into a caste, for class and caste, so to say, are next door neighbours, and it is only a span that separates the two. **A caste is an enclosed class.**

The study of the origin of caste must furnish us with an answer to the question—what is the class that raised this "enclosure" around itself? The question [pg 89] may seem too inquisitorial, but it is pertinent, and an answer to this will serve us to elucidate the mystery of the growth and development of castes all over India. Unfortunately a direct answer to this question is not within my power. I can answer it only indirectly. I said just above that the customs in question were current in the Hindu society. To be true to facts it is necessary to qualify the statement, as it connotes universality of their prevalence. These customs in all their strictness are obtainable only in one caste, namely the Brahmans, who occupy the highest place in the social hierarchy of the Hindu society; and as their prevalence in Non-Brahman castes is derivative their observance is neither strict nor complete. This important fact can serve as a basis of an important observation. If the prevalence of these customs in the non-Brahman Castes is derivative, as can be shown very easily, then it needs no argument to prove what class is the father of the institution of caste. Why the Brahman class should have enclosed itself into a caste is a different question, which may be left as an employment for another occasion. But the strict observance of these customs and the social superiority arrogated by the priestly class in all ancient civilizations are sufficient to prove that they were the originators of this “unnatural institution” founded and maintained through these unnatural means.

I now come to the third part of my paper regarding the question of the growth and spread of the caste system all over India. The question I have to answer is: How did the institution of caste spread among the rest of the non-Brahman population of the country? The question of the spread of the castes all over India has suffered a worse fate than the question of genesis. And the main cause, as it seems to me, is that the two questions of spread and of origin are not separated. This is because of the common belief among scholars that the caste system has either been imposed upon the docile population of India by a law-giver as a divine dispensation, or that it has grown according to some law of social growth peculiar to the Indian people.

I first propose to handle the law-giver of India. Every country has its lawgiver, who arises as an incarnation (*avatar*) in times of emergency to set right a sinning humanity and give it the laws of justice and morality. Manu, the law-giver of India, if he did exist, was certainly an audacious person. If the story that he gave the law of caste be credited, then Manu must have been a dare-devil fellow and the humanity that accepted his dispensation must be a humanity quite different from the one we are acquainted with. It is unimaginable that the law of caste was *given.* It is hardly an exaggeration to say that Manu could not have outlived his law, for what is that class that can submit to be degraded to the status of brutes by the pen of a man, and suffer him to raise another class to the pinnacle? Unless he was a tyrant who held all the population in subjection it cannot be imagined that he could have been allowed to dispense his patronage in this grossly unjust manner, as may be easily seen by a mere glance at his "Institutes." I may seem hard on Manu, but I am sure my force is not strong enough to kill his ghost. He lives, like a disembodied spirit and is appealed to, and I am afraid will yet live long. One thing I want to impress upon you is that Manu did not *give* the *law* of Caste and that he could not do so. Caste existed long before Manu. He was an upholder of it and therefore philosophised about it, but certainly he did not and could not ordain the present order of Hindu Society. His work ended with the codification of existing caste rules and the preaching of Caste *Dharma*. The spread and growth of the Caste system is too [pg 90] gigantic a task to be achieved by the power or cunning of an individual or of a class. Similar in argument is the theory that the Brahmans created the caste. After what I have said regarding Manu, I need hardly say anything more, except to point out that it is incorrect in thought and malicious in intent. The Brahmans may have been guilty of many things, and I dare say they are, but the imposing of the caste system on the non-Brahman population was beyond their mettle. They may have helped the process by their glib philosophy, but they certainly could not have pushed their scheme beyond their own confines. To fashion society after one's own pattern! How glorious! How hard! One can take pleasure and eulogize its furtherance, but cannot further it very far. The vehemence of my attack may seem to be unnecessary: but I can assure you that it is not uncalled for. There is a strong belief in the mind of orthodox Hindus that the Hindu Society was somehow moulded into the frame work of the Caste System, and that it is an organization consciously created by the *Shâstras*. Not only does this belief exist, but it is being justified on the ground that it cannot but be good, because it is ordained by the *Shâstras* and the *Shâstras* cannot be wrong. I have urged so much on the adverse side of this attitude, not because the religious sanctity is grounded on scientific basis, nor to help those reformers who are preaching against it. Preaching did not make the caste system, neither will it unmake it. My aim is to show the falsity of the attitude that has exalted religious sanction to the position of a scientific explanation.

Thus the great man theory does not help us very far in solving the spread of castes in India. Western scholars, probably not much given to hero-worship, have attempted other explanations. The nuclei, round which have "formed" the various castes in India, are, according to them:—(1) occupation; (2) survivals of tribal organizations, etc.; (3) the rise of new belief; (4) cross-breeding and (5) migration.

The question may be asked whether these nuclei do not exist in other societies and whether they are peculiar to India. If they are not peculiar to India, but are common to the world, why is it that they did not "form" caste on other parts of this planet? Is it because those parts are holier than the land of the Vedas, or that the professors are mistaken? I am afraid that the latter is the truth.

Inspite of the high theoretic value claimed by the several authors for their respective theories, based on one or other of the above nuclei, one regrets to say that on close examination they are nothing more than filling illustrations—what Matthew Arnold means by "the grand name without the grand thing in it." Such are the various theories of caste advanced by Sir Denzil Ibbetson, Mr. Nesfield, M. Senart and Sir H. Risley. To criticise them in a lump would be to say that they are a disguised form of the *Petitio Principii* of formal logic. To illustrate: Mr. Nesfield says that "function and function only ... was the foundation upon which the whole system of castes in India was built up." But he may rightly be reminded that he does not very much advance our thought by making the above statement, which practically amounts to saying that castes in India are functional or occupational, which is a very poor discovery! We have yet to know from Mr. Nesfield why is it that an occupational group turned into an occupational caste? I would very cheerfully have undertaken the task of dwelling on the [pg 91] theories of other ethnologists, had it not been for the fact that Mr. Nesfield's is a typical one.

Without stopping to criticize those theories that explain the caste system as a natural phenomenon occurring in obedience to the law of disintegration, as explained by Herbert Spencer in his formula of evolution, or as natural as "the structural differentiation within an organism"—to employ the phraseology of orthodox apologists—, or as an early attempt to test the laws of eugenics—as all belonging to the same class of fallacy which regards the caste system as inevitable, or as being consciously imposed in anticipation of these laws on a helpless and humble population, I will now lay before you my own view on the subject.

We shall be well advised to recall at the outset that the Hindu society, in common with other societies, was composed of classes and the earliest known are the (1) Brahmans or the priestly class: (2) the Kshatriya, or the military class: (3) the Vaiśya, or the merchant class: and (4) the Sudra, or the artisan and menial class. Particular attention has to be paid to the fact that this was essentially a class system, in which individuals, when qualified, could change their class, and therefore classes did change their personnel. At some time in the history of the Hindus, the priestly class socially detached itself from the rest of the body of people and through a closed-door policy became a caste by itself. The other classes being subject to the law of social division of labour underwent differentiation, some into large, others into very minute groups. The Vaiśya and Sudra classes were the original inchoate plasm, which formed the sources of the numerous castes of to-day. As the military occupation does not very easily lend itself to very minute sub-division, the Kshatriya class could have differentiated into soldiers and administrators.

This sub-division of a society is quite natural. But the unnatural thing about these sub-divisions is that they have lost the open door character of the class system and have become self-enclosed units called castes. The question is, were they compelled to close their doors and become endogamous, or did they close them of their own accord? I submit that there is a double line of answer: **Some closed the door: others found it closed against them**. The one is a psychological interpretation and the other is mechanistic, but they are complementary and both are necessary to explain the phenomena of caste formation in its entirety.

I will first take up the psychological interpretation. The question we have to answer in this connection is: Why did these sub-divisions or classes, if you please, industrial, religious or otherwise, become self-enclosed or endogamous? My answer is because the Brahmans were so. Endogamy, or the closed-door system, was a fashion in the Hindu Society, and as it had originated from the Brahman caste it was whole-heartedly imitated by all the non-Brahman sub-divisions or classes, who, in their turn, became endogamous castes. It is "the infection of imitation" that caught all these sub-divisions on their onward march of differentiation and has turned them into castes. The propensity to imitate is a deep-seated one in the human mind and need not be deemed an inadequate explanation for the formation of the various castes in India. It is so deep-seated that Walter Bagehot argues that "we must not think of ... imitation as voluntary, or even conscious. On the contrary it has its seat mainly in very obscure parts of the mind, whose notions, so far from being consciously produced, are hardly felt to exist; so far from being conceived beforehand, are not even felt at the time. The main seat of the imitative part of our nature is our belief, and the causes predisposing us to believe this or disinclining us to believe that are among the obscurest parts of our nature. But as to the imitative nature [pg 92] of credulity there can be no doubt."[4] This propensity to imitate has been made the subject of a scientific study by Gabriel Tarde, who lays down three laws of imitation. One of his three laws is that imitation flows from the higher to the lower or, to quote his own words, "Given the opportunity, a nobility will always and everywhere imitate its leaders, its kings or sovereigns, and the people likewise, given the opportunity, its nobility."[5] Another of Tarde's laws of imitation is: that the extent or intensity of imitation varies inversely in proportion to distance, or in his own words "the thing that is most imitated is the most superior one of those that are nearest. In fact, the influence of the model's example is efficacious inversely to its *distance* as well as directly to its superiority. Distance is understood here in its sociological meaning. However distant in space a stranger may be, he is close by, from this point of view, if we have numerous and daily relations with him and if we have every facility to satisfy our desire to imitate him. This law of the imitation of the nearest, of the least distant, explains the gradual and consecutive

---

4 Physics and Politics 1915, p. 60.

5 Laws of Imitation, Tr. by E. C. Parsons, 2nd ed. p. 217.

character of the spread of an example that has been set by the higher social ranks."[6]

In order to prove my thesis—which really needs no proof—that some castes were formed by imitation, the best way, it seems to me, is to find out whether or not the vital conditions for the formation of castes by imitation exist in the Hindu Society. The conditions for imitation, according to this standard authority are: (1) That the source of imitation must enjoy prestige in the group and (2) that there must be "numerous and daily relations" among members of a group. That these conditions were present in India there is little reason to doubt. The Brahman is a semi-god and very nearly a demi-god. He sets up a mode and moulds the rest. His prestige is unquestionable and is the fountain-head of bliss and good. Can such a being, idolised by Scriptures and venerated by the priest-ridden multitude, fail to project his personality on the suppliant humanity? Why, if the story be true, he is believed to be the very end of creation. Such a creature is worthy of more than mere imitation, but at least of imitation; and if he lives in an endogamous enclosure, should not the rest follow his example? Frail humanity! Be it embodied in a grave philosopher or a frivolous housemaid, it succumbs. It cannot be otherwise. Imitation is easy and invention is difficult.

---

[6] Ibid. p. 224.

Yet another way of demonstrating the play of imitation in the formation of castes is to understand the attitude of non-Brahman classes towards those customs which supported the structure of caste in its nascent days until, in the course of history, it became embedded in the Hindu mind and hangs there to this day without any support—for now it needs no prop but belief—like a weed on the surface of a pond. In a way, but only in a way, the status of a caste in the Hindu Society varies directly with the extent of the observance of the customs of *sati*, enforced widowhood, and girl marriage. But observance of these customs varies directly with the *distance* (I am using the word in the Tardian sense) that separates the caste. Those castes that are nearest to the Brahmans have imitated all the three customs and insist on the strict observance thereof. Those that are less near have imitated enforced widowhood and girl marriage; others, a little further off, have only girl marriage, and those furthest off have imitated only the belief in the caste principle. This imperfect imitation, I dare say, is due partly to what Tarde calls "distance" and partly to the barbarous character of these customs. This [pg 93] phenomenon is a complete illustration of Tarde's law and leaves no doubt that the whole process of caste-formation in India is a process of imitation of the higher by the lower. At this juncture I will turn back to support a former conclusion of mine, which might have appeared to you as too sudden or unsupported. I said that the Brahman class first raised the structure of caste by the help of those three customs in question. My reason for that conclusion was that their existence in other classes was derivative. After what I have said regarding the rôle of imitation in the spread of these customs among the non-Brahman castes, as means or as ideals, though the imitators have not been aware of it, they exist among them as derivatives; and, if they are derived, there must have been prevalent one original caste that was high enough to have served as a pattern for the rest. But in a theocratic society, who could be the pattern but the servant of God?

This completes the story of those that were weak enough to close their doors. Let us now see how others were closed in as a result of being closed out. This I call the mechanistic process of the formation of caste. It is mechanistic because it is inevitable. That this line of approach, as well as the psychological one, to the explanation of the subject has escaped my predecessors is entirely due to the fact that they have conceived Caste as a unit by itself and not as one within a System of Caste. The result of this oversight or lack of sight has been very detrimental to the proper understanding of the subject matter and therefore its correct explanation. I will proceed to offer my own explanation by making one remark which I will urge you to bear constantly in mind. It is this: that **caste in the singular number is an unreality**.

Castes exist only in the plural number. There is no such thing as *a* caste: there are always castes. To illustrate my meaning: while making themselves into a caste, the Brahmans, by virtue of this, created a non-Brahman caste; or, to express it in my own way, while closing themselves in they closed others out. I will clear my point by taking another illustration. Take India as a whole with its various communities designated by the various creeds to which they owe allegiance, to wit, the Hindus, Muhammadans, Jews, Christians and Parsis. Now, barring the Hindus, the rest within themselves are non-caste communities. But with respect to each other they are castes. Again, if the first four enclose themselves, the Parsis are directly closed out, but are indirectly closed in. Symbolically, if group A. wants to be endogamous, group B. has to be so by sheer force of circumstances.

Now apply the same logic to the Hindu society and you have another explanation of the "fissiparous" character of caste, as a consequence of the virtue of self-duplication that is inherent in it. Any innovation that seriously antagonises the ethical, religious and social code of the Caste is not likely to be tolerated by the Caste, and the recalcitrant members of a Caste are in danger of being thrown out of the Caste, and left to their own fate without having the alternative of being admitted into or absorbed by other Castes. Caste rules are inexorable and they do not wait to make nice distinctions between kinds of offence. Innovation may be of any kind, but all kinds will suffer the same penalty. A novel way of thinking will create a new Caste for the old ones will not tolerate it. The noxious thinker respectfully called Guru (Prophet) suffers the same fate as the sinners in illegitimate love. The former creates a caste of the nature of a religious sect and the latter a type of mixed caste. Castes have no mercy for a sinner who has the courage to violate the code. The penalty is excommunication and the result is a new caste. It is not peculiar Hindu psychology that induces the excommunicated to form themselves into a caste: far from it. On the contrary, very often they have been quite [pg 94] willing to be humble members of some caste (higher by preference) if they could be admitted within its fold. But castes are enclosed units and it is their conspiracy with clear conscience that compels the excommunicated to make themselves into a caste. The logic of this obdurate circumstance is merciless, and it is in obedience to its force that some unfortunate groups find themselves enclosed, because others in enclosing, themselves have closed them out, with the result that new groups (formed on any basis obnoxious to the caste rules) by a mechanical law are constantly being converted into castes to a bewildering multiplicity. Thus is told the second tale in the process of Caste formation in India.

Now to summarise the main points of my thesis. In my opinion there have been several mistakes committed by the students of Caste, which have misled them in their investigations. European students of Caste have unduly emphasised the rôle of colour in the caste-system. Themselves impregnated by colour prejudices, they very readily imagined it to be the chief factor in the Caste problem. But nothing can be farther from the truth, and Dr. Ketkar is correct when he insists that "All the princes whether they belonged to the so-called Aryan race, or the so-called Dravidian race, were Aryas. Whether a tribe or a family was racially Aryan or Dravidian was a question which never troubled the people of India, until foreign scholars came in and began to draw the line. The colour of the skin had long ceased to be a matter of importance."[7] Again, they have mistaken mere descriptions for explanation and fought over them as though they were theories of origin. There are occupational, religious, etc. castes, it is true, but it is by no means an explanation of the origin of Caste. We have yet to find out why occupational groups are castes; but this question has never even been raised. Lastly they have taken Caste very lightly as though a breath had made it. On the contrary, Caste, as I have explained it, is almost impossible to be sustained: for the difficulties that it involves are tremendous. It is true that Caste rests on belief, but before belief comes to be the foundation of an institution, the institution itself needs to be perpetuated and fortified. My study of the Caste problem involves four main points: (1)

---

[7] History of Caste p. 82.

That in spite of the composite make-up of the Hindu population, there is a deep cultural unity. (2) That Caste is a parcelling into bits of a larger cultural unit. (3) That there was one Caste to start with. (4) That classes have become Castes through imitation and excommunication.

Peculiar interest attaches to the problem of Caste in India to-day, as persistent attempts are being made to do away with this unnatural institution. Such attempts at reform, however, have aroused a great deal of controversy regarding its origin, as to whether it is due to the conscious command of a Supreme Authority, or is an unconscious growth in the life of a human society under peculiar circumstances. Those who hold the latter view will, I hope, find some food for thought in the standpoint adopted in this paper. Apart from its practical importance the subject of Caste is an all absorbing problem and the interest aroused in me regarding its theoretic foundations has moved me to put before you some of the conclusions, which seem to me well founded, and the grounds upon which they may be supported. I am not, however, so presumptuous as to think them in any way final, or anything more than a contribution to a discussion of the subject. It seems to me that the car has been shunted on wrong lines, and the primary object of the paper is to indicate what I regard to be the right path of investigation, with a view to arrive at a serviceable truth. We must, however, guard against approaching the subject with a bias.

[pg 95] Sentiment must be outlawed from the domain of science and things should be judged from an objective standpoint. For myself I shall find as much pleasure in a positive destruction of my own ideology, as in a rational disagreement on a topic, which, notwithstanding many learned disquisitions is likely to remain controversial for ever. To conclude, while I am ambitious to advance a Theory of Caste, if it can be shown to be untenable I shall be equally willing to give it up.